I0533450

Cover Art by Mairena

Cover Design by Unfortunate Designs

Independently Published by Unfortunate Productions LLC

Print ISBN: 979-8-9913742-4-8

Taking a
Tumble

Clover Holloway

BLURB

Kaz want's nothing more than his very own meet-cute with Tabitha, a human, but he seems to only run into her when he's at his worst. He's content to pine from afar, he is an older demon with a dad-bod after all. There's no way someone as gorgeous as Tabi would look his way.

Tabi loves visiting Ruff N' Tumble. There are so many cute animals you'd never find anywhere else, but if she's honest with herself, its the shop's owner she wants to take home.

Follow along as Kaz and Tabi bumble their way into their happily ever after, complete with animal shenanigans and unusual encounters.

Set in Ghostlight Falls, the coolest fictional small town in the Pacific Northwest, *Taking a Tumble* is a standalone cozy paranormal novella with wholesome Hallmark movie vibes and a good amount of steam.

DEDICATION

To Arlo.

CONTENT CONSIDERATIONS

This is a fictional paranormal novella where there is more smut than plot. Adult themes and contents to consider include but are not limited to adult language, cute animals, a MMC with two c-cks, oral schmex (fellatio and cunnilingus), penetrative schmex, peen piercings, nip nop piercings, sp@nking, squ-rting, dirty talk, sexting, unprotected schmex, horn play, insta-lust, a mischievous foxkin, and a turtle in a bow tie.

CHAPTER 1
A TUMBLE INDEED
KAZ'RON

If you'd have asked me ten years ago where I thought I'd be now, it sure wouldn't be ass-first in a puddle of mud, holding a leash, being judged by the pristine cream foxkin who's led me on a wild goose chase for the past forty-five minutes. I swear to god she's judging me right now.

A stifled laugh from above follows the appearance of feminine legs clad in ripped jeans.

This day just keeps getting better.

I don't have to look to know who it is, but I drag my gaze up her gorgeous form, trying not to spend too long detailing the complex floral tattoos on her arm before I meet her eyes.

Tabitha.

If my skin wasn't already red, I'm sure my cheeks

would be flaming in embarrassment. Tabitha bends down and the foxkin–that traitor–hops happily into her arms, settling against her breast and purring.

Yeah, okay, I'd do the same thing if I had the opportunity.

"Rough day?" Tabi's eyes shine with mirth as she pets the sinister critter's cream colored fur.

Rolling to my knees, I push myself up with a great amount of effort until I'm standing. I'm not a spring chicken anymore, my joints aren't as limber as they used to be. Turning toward Tabitha, I wipe my hands on my jeans in a futile effort to clean myself up a little.

"Ah, yeah. You could say that," I mutter. Words have never come easy to me around the feisty woman in front of me. I've had the biggest crush on Tabi since she moved to Ghostlight Falls last year. 'Crush' sounds so juvenile, but that's what it is. It's also less creepy than *infatuation*.

She's younger than I am—in her mid 30s—but age is just a number, right? She leans forward to grab the leash off the ground, and her supple tits are suddenly in my face.

Holy Hades. Tabi's not small. She's a grown woman with curves I desperately want to sink my fingers—and maybe my teeth—into. Her breasts are pushed above the dip in her v-neck shirt, and I want to bless and curse whoever invented whatever bra she's wearing.

My dicks twitch and I know I need to look away before I make this situation even more awkward than it already is. She doesn't need to see me sweaty, covered in mud, *and* sporting a double boner.

My brain comes back online and I realize I shouldn't be making her handle the foxkin, so I reach for the leash, too. Our fingers brush as we both take a hold of the rope at the same time, and a spark of electricity and longing gets mainlined to my heart. Her eyes meet mine, she hitches a breath—I think. This would be the perfect meet-cute, every Hallmark movie come to life—if I was cool and confident.

Unfortunately, I'm not. At all. In fact, I'd hazard to say I am what the kids call *awkward AF*. At least I heard my niece say something like that. The result is that instead of stroking my thumb over her pulse point, or leaning in to claim her lips, I jerk backward abruptly, lose my balance, and fall *back* in the mud puddle.

Tabitha smoothly clips the leash to the foxkin's collar, biting her plump lower lip as she tries to stifle a laugh. Her eyes light with mirth, and she's so fucking pretty that my humiliation fades into something more akin to amusement. If my unfortunate escapades bring her joy, then at least the experience was worth it.

"So, how does this cutie keep getting out?" Tabitha questions, and I'm brought back to reality. She hands me the leash, and I put my wrist through the loop before gripping the length of cord tightly. I am not taking any chances that this creature will get away from me again...today anyway.

I look at the foxkin in question. *Is she smirking at me?*

"She has been taking advantage of new customers who aren't familiar with her species. I warn them that she's crafty before I take her out for them to pet, but she always manages to jump away from them when they let their guard down. I swear, I'll never have another foxkin. This one was a mistake."

Tabi laughs, and the sound is downright magical. "A cute mistake."

"She knows it, too," I grumble.

A hand appears in front of my face, and I realize it's Tabitha's. She's offering me help. Help I gladly accept because I'm not an alpha male willing to pass up the opportunity to touch a beautiful woman in the name of being manly.

Her grip tightens, and with strength I couldn't have predicted, she yanks me up. Unfortunately since I wasn't expecting it, I'm unable to counter the force she put into that pull, and my momentum shoves me until I'm falling against Tabi.

For a moment, I'm stunned. Our bodies are touching. I can smell faint traces of mango from her shampoo. Mortification sets in as I look down, and realize I am covering poor Tabi in mud. The foxkin smushed between us wriggles with fervor until she escapes and leaps to the ground. The creature immediately begins cleaning herself, sending dirty looks my way as she does.

Serves you right for running from me, you little menace.

I don't say that out loud, though. I'm too busy chastising myself for making an already embarrassing situation worse.

"Oh, gods, Tabitha! I am so sorry. I didn't mean to...you're just...shit, here." Words vomit from my mouth in no coherent order as I pull off my open flannel shirt and begin wiping the mud off of the woman in front of me. Only when the body beneath my palms begins to vibrate do I pause.

Tabi is laughing. Soft, like she doesn't want to disturb me. It's then I realize that my attempt to clean Tabitha up has me stroking my ruined shirt across her breasts. My eyes widen in horror as they meet her amused ones.

Her tits may as well be made from lava based on how fast I jump back, tearing my hand from her body. One glance at them reveals hard-tipped nipples pushing through the fabric of her shirt. Frozen once more, I shake my head to clear it.

"Fuck! Tabi. I...um...I'm sorry. I shouldn't have...oh gods. I just...uh...thanks for your help. Have a great day!" The last words are nearly a squeak and I reach for the foxkin's leash, yank it from Tabitha's hands, and turn to speed-walk back to the shop.

Talk about a walk of shame. I'm such a fucking coward.

CHAPTER 2
DEMON FANTASIES
TABI

A smile breaks free as I watch Kaz run away from me, sneaking a peek at his mud-covered ass. I'm not usually a butt gal, but for him I'd make an exception.

I'm not sure why he gets so flustered around me. It's actually kind of adorable. The demon is definitely attracted to me, if the bulge that was trying to bust through the zipper on his jeans is any indication.

A bell tinkles as he opens the door to his shop, Ruff 'N Tumble, and drags the foxkin inside. He may think she's a menace, but I'm thankful for her antics today. That's the most facetime I've gotten with Kaz, and I even got a little heavy petting out of it. Accidental, but I'll take it.

I turn and walk back toward my apartment. I'm now covered in mud thanks to our little run-in, and I need to get back to work anyway. The client I'm working with is so needy, and the faster I'm done with this project, the better.

As I walk, I take in the sights surrounding me. Grim, the baker, is putting loaves of fresh bread into the window. Mina is chasing a rogue chicken over at Birds of a Feather Chicken Rescue. Ghostlight Falls is a small town full of unusual characters, but it's also overflowing with whimsy. So different from LA where I grew up. The pace here is slower, calmer. Exactly what I needed.

I've been here nearly a year now, and I truly consider this place home. I'd like to settle here permanently if the stars align. Of course, it doesn't hurt that a certain red-skinned hottie is a resident of the town.

Climbing the steps to my unit, I unlock the door and sweep inside. I pull off my sullied top as I walk to the bathroom, throwing it onto the pile by the closet. A quick flick of the tap and the water is on and warming. I strip the rest of the way down as the shower fills with steam, throw my hair into a messy bun, then step under the deliciously hot spray. For a moment, I just stand there. Eyes closed, arms wrapped around my body as I let the water heat me to my bones.

No need to wash my hair, I did that last night and gods know I'm not about to do it more than necessary. This rinse is simply to get the mud off. I grab a wash-cloth and dampen it before swiping across my chest.

Except the act makes me think of Kaz trying to clean me up, his large hands wiping that soft flannel across my breasts. A twinge of arousal makes itself known between my legs, and my nipples beg to be touched.

Who am I to deny my body? This shower doesn't have the greatest water pressure—trust me, I've tried—but my fingers do a fine enough job. Turning to lean against the cold tile, I let the warm spray run down my body and close my eyes. The juxtaposition of temperatures already has my skin on high alert, so when I smooth my hands up my stomach to cup my breasts, a moan slips from my lips.

What if Kaz had kept going, rubbing lower? Maybe beneath the hem of my shirt, brushing those calloused fingers over my nipples. Fuck, he doesn't know I have them pierced. Would he like that? Maybe tug on the barbell of one while he spins the other with his wet tongue?

I tug on the jewelry lightly, imagining Kaz doing it instead. My clit throbs with each pull, so I slide one hand down between my legs, a finger gliding through my slit to rub the swollen nub.

"Fuck!" I shout before I can catch myself, then bite my lip to stop it from happening again. Abandoning my other breast, I spread myself open so I can rub circles over my clit, getting harder with each pass. My breathing speeds, the water still sluicing down my body giving me extra sensation.

I've heard some demons have two cocks. Of course, I haven't had the chance to see the phenomenon for myself, but based on the size of Kaz's bulge, the rumors don't lie. I've always wanted to try double penetration, but I don't have the lady-balls to have a threesome. This would be the perfect solution.

Shoving two fingers into my pussy, I imagine what it would feel like to be filled in both holes. I wish I had the flexibility to simulate it. Or, oh gods, what if he thrust both his cocks in my pussy at the same time? The stretch would be unreal. Maybe he'd take me from behind, filling me up completely while he twists my nipples and...

"Ah! Kaz!" The orgasm hits me out of nowhere. I mean, I know that was my end goal, but usually I have more build up. The fantasy was just that fucking hot that it catapulted me over the edge.

Blinking my eyes open to join the real world again, I pull my fingers from my pussy. It clenches around nothing at the loss, the aftershocks of that epic climax still running through my system. I haven't come that hard in a long ass time, especially not using just my hands. The water is luke-warm now, but I bear it to rinse myself clean of my own cum before shutting off the tap and grabbing a fluffy towel. My muscles are still languid from the hot water and the pleasure, and my mind can't help but wander to the demon who owns the pet shop.

Maybe I'll have to be the one to make the first move. I'm not usually that girl, but we've been dancing around each other for months, and he seems shyer than me.

Thoughts of Kaz continue to float through my mind as I move onto the rest of my post-shower routine. I'm so glad when I bought linens for my new place that I splurged on the "bath sheet" size towels. I'm not a small woman, regular towels just don't cover my curves. This one may as well be a robe it swallows me so completely.

Towel wrapped around my body, I work leave-in conditioner into my hair. How would it feel to have Kaz run his fingers through the strands, maybe he'd grip it in his fists while he fucked my fa—

Oh. My. Gods. That's it, I can't keep fantasizing about the poor man. I either need to woman-up and ask him out, or find new spank bank material. Drifting to my underwear drawer, my gaze zeros in on the black lacy bra I rarely wear, and I come to a decision. Grabbing the bra and matching panties—because a matching set always boosts my confidence—I pick out a tank top with a *deep* v and my high-waisted shorts.

Fuck all this running around. It's time to woman-up.

CHAPTER 3

GOTTA BE MAGIC

KAZ'RON

"Here you are," I say, handing the travel cage with a young lupig over to Mrs. Robinson. "Don't forget! Just a small handful of feed a day. We don't want this little guy getting too fat! Lupig's are notoriously greedy. Don't fall for the sad eyes."

Mrs. Robinson chuffs a laugh, then walks out the front door of Ruff 'N Tumble, causing the bell to ring. I really hope she heeds my instructions, there's nothing wrong with a few extra pounds, but lupigs will get rounder than they are tall if you aren't careful. Cute as fuck, but very temperamental.

Looking around the store, I see a red balloon drifting down the aisle toward me.

"Hello, Arlo!" I coo once the balloon has reached

the front counter. Arlo is a turtle of sorts, but not like the ones you usually find in the human realm. He came from the demon-realm with me when I moved to Ghostlight Falls. His red skin complements my own, and his horns are similar as well. It's his bright turquoise shell that's the real show stopper, though.

He loves to wander, and I always worry he's going to get into trouble or escape, but he abhors being caged in. That's why I tie a balloon around his shell every morning when we're at the shop. This way, Arlo can wander to his heart's content, but I always know where he is. It's a huge hit with the customers also. He's a town favorite.

I crouch down when Arlo butts his tiny head into my shin. "More scratchies? You're a greedy little thing aren't you?" He burrows his head into my open palm, a sign of affection. I chuckle. "Gods, you'd never survive in the wild."

Good thing he won't have to. He's stuck with me for life.

The bell above the door tinkles, signaling a new customer has entered the shop. Pushing on my quads to rise, my knee pops embarrassingly loud. I go to greet the new entrant and freeze.

It's her. Tabitha. And Holyyyyy Fuck. What the hell is she wearing? Is she trying to send me to an early grave? I swear I'm having heart palpitations just looking at her. Am I drooling? I'm probably drooling.

White shorts show off an expanse of tan skin and thick thighs I want wrapped around my ears. Her top is borderline scandalous, dipping so low it reveals new freckles on her breasts I've never seen before. And fuck me, is that lace? It is. The edge of her black lace bra is just visible in the shirt's gap.

Realizing I've been staring like a creeper, I whip my eyes to meet hers. A smug grin grows into a full blown smile when our eyes lock, and I'm absolutely positive she knows I was checking her out. But can you blame a man? A woman like her coming in here looking like that? I have no choice but to stare. Respectfully, of course.

Though there are some *very* disrespectful things I'd like to do to this woman.

Tabitha's hands land on the counter between us, and thank gods it is because that double-boner? There's no hiding it now. Finally, I gather enough brain cells to speak.

"Hey," I cough because the word came out as a squeak, like a youngling before their balls have dropped. "Um, hey, uh, Tabitha. What brings you in here today? Looking for a new friend?" There. That was acceptable. Hopefully.

"Mmm, yeah you could say that." Tabi purrs.

It takes an embarrassing amount of mental fortitude to continue like she isn't a walking wet dream. "Well, uh, we have several options in right now. Some lupigs, a couple karakeets, that naughty foxkin you helped me catch earlier..." I trail off.

"Oh I am definitely looking for a naughty friend, but maybe something a little more...manly."

Manly? What could she possibly mean by that? She doesn't mean...no. My brain is just frazzled from the way the word naughty rolled off her plush lips. Does she mean a tougher animal?

"Okayyyy, If you're looking for a stronger pet, can I ask what it's for? It will help me narrow down some options for you. Is it for protection or—"

Her hand grazing the top of mine cuts me off mid tangent. Tabi giggles and bites her lip, and I think I may be hallucinating the next words out of her mouth.

"Kaz, I'm talking about you. I'm trying—unsuccessfully—to seduce you to come on a date with me."

When I say nothing, her face falls, insecurity flashing over her features. She steps back, my hand left cold when she pulls hers away to wring it with its partner in front of her.

"Oh gods," she starts. "I... I thought...oh I've read this all wrong haven't I?" She's backing away from me now and it's the last thing I want. "I'm so sorry, Kaz. Please forget this ever happened. I...shit—"

"No!" She stops in her tracks when I yell. "I mean, yes! No, don't leave! Yes, a date!" *Real eloquent there, Kaz, totally nailing this interaction.*

I take a deep breath and try again. "I was just a little shocked that a gorgeous woman like you would even be interested in someone like me. But, please, let me take you on a date. I promise I'm not this weird and awkward all the time." That's a straight up lie, but for her, I'll try.

Her expression lights up, and I can't help but puff my chest a little that I wiped that melancholy look off her face. She steps forward once more.

"I'm the one who asked you out, remember?" She teases.

"You made the first move, let me reward you for your bravery. Maybe this weekend? Are you free Saturday?" I'm not sure where this confidence is coming from, but I will it not to stop now.

Tabi nods. "I can do Saturday. Here, let me give you my number so you can text me the details."

After a quick scramble to dig my phone from my pocket, I lay it in her waiting palm and watch in awe as she inputs her phone number and texts herself so she has mine as well. With a smile, Tabitha hands me the device back, then digs her hands in her back pockets and backs away from the counter. Her cheeks are flushed pink, but she is nearly bouncing on her toes from excitement or happiness—maybe both.

"Saturday. It's a date! See ya, Kaz."

"Uh, yeah. See ya," is the best response I can

muster. She swans out the door, the overhead bell tinkling once again, but this time it sounds magical. Because never in my wildest dreams would I have ever thought the woman I have been pining after for a year would waltz in here and ask me out.

Yeah. Gotta be magic.

CHAPTER 4
A VERY GOOD GASP!
TABI

"**B**ut what do I wear?" I whine to Hannah, my best friend who's face stares back at me from my phone propped on my dresser as we video call.

"Well, what are you guys doing?" she asks, logical as ever.

"I don't know! He just said it was outside and to wear comfy shoes." I lament.

"Okayyyyy," she starts, "how about that cute floral romper, the one with the thin straps? That way you have the look of a dress but the protection of shorts if he takes you on some daredevil experience. Plus you can wear your Chucks with it. Cute and comfortable."

I laugh at her reasoning. "I don't think we'll be going on any 'daredevil experiences,' but the romper is a great idea. You're a genius, Han."

A deep sigh comes from the phone. "I know. What would you do without me?"

"I'd be a spinster stuck at home with seventeen cats and a penchant for spinning my own yarn." I deadpan back before noticing what time it is on the little clock over Hannah's head.

"Oh shit! Okay, gotta go. He's gonna be here in less than twenty minutes. Fuck, I'm not ready. Bye!"

I hang up on my best friend and get my butt into gear getting ready for our date. I don't know why I'm so nervous, but the butterflies in my stomach are having some kind of Irish jig competition and I'd really like it if they'd settle down.

Just as I'm tying my second sneaker, a knock sounds at my front door.

"Ah! He's here!" I stand abruptly, run to the mirror, swipe a little lipgloss on and fluff my hair, then rush to the door, slowing at the last second to seem like I'm calm as a cucumber. Spoiler alert: I'm not. I just really want this date to go well. It's been so long since I've been on one, and even longer since I was this invested in the outcome.

With one last fortifying breath, I swing open the door.

Instead of a handsome red face, I see a huge bouquet of flowers, a set of horns peeking out above the blooms. I can't help but smile.

"Hi! I assume there's a Kaz'ron somewhere back there?" I tease.

The flowers rapidly disappear from my line of sight and the handsome demon gives me a sheepish look.

"Uh, sorry. Hi. Uh, these are for you!" Kaz trips over his words as he thrusts the blooms in my direction. I have to hold back a laugh because he's so damn awkward but it's incredibly endearing. He isn't putting on airs or trying to be someone he's not. Finally, I put him out of his misery, taking the flowers from him and stepping aside, motioning with my other hand for him to come in.

"Let me just get a vase for these before we go." I head to the kitchen, then pause and look back over my shoulder. "Thank you, Kaz'ron."

A small smile tugs at the corners of his lips as he replies, "Kaz. You can call me Kaz."

Arranging the lovely assortment of sunflowers, Alstroemeria, and Gerbera daisies, I yell out to him from the kitchen. "So, Kaz," I make sure to draw out his nickname since he asked me to call him that. "Where are we going for our date?"

He waits to answer until I'm walking back into the living room. "I thought we could go to the park. There's a cover band playing 90's songs."

I can't help it, I gasp. Kaz eyes me warily.

"Is that a good gasp or a bad gasp?" he asks.

"A good gasp! A very good gasp! I love live music and the 90's are my jam." I'm so genuinely excited I'm nearly bouncing on my toes, and Kaz's face lights up at my enthusiasm. I grab his hand and tug him toward the door. "Let's go!"

CHAPTER 5

THE HOLEY WONDERS

KAZ'RON

I can't believe I'm here with Tabitha. After months of pining after the woman, all it took was a foxkin mishap to nudge things along. When I told her the plan for tonight's date, I thought she may vibrate out of her skin. The way her face lit up and she reached for my hand—I swear that's a core memory now.

A crisp fall breeze wafts the scents of spiked cider and fried food toward us, as we walk the lane leading up to the park. Music follows, though not the band just yet. They must be playing some filler music while people arrive and get settled.

We chatted on the short walk here. Nothing monumental, just easy get-to-know-you questions. The blanket I brought for us to sit on is under my right arm, Tabi's hand holding my left. Yeah, I'm still in awe of that, too. She grabbed my hand at her apartment and never let go. The initial spark when she first made contact has faded to a warm contentment. She did it so naturally, like we'd held hands a million times before. It's like she doesn't have an awkward bone in her body.

"Where would you like to sit?" I ask her as we finally make it to the grassy area in front of the stage. Vendors surround the edges of the park, ready to peddle their wares to concert-goers. Tabi looks around, surveying the open areas.

"Maybe over there? It's a little further back, but we won't be at risk of being stepped on." She points to an empty nook near the back of the field, pretty far from the stage but where we can still see it.

"That's perfect," I say. "Not going to lie, I'm a bit of an old man and would rather not be up near the stage anyway. Though I would have done it for you," I amend. There's a lot I would do for this woman. Maybe not any major crimes, but honestly? It depends on the situation.

Tabi shoots me a winning smile as we make our way to the spot she's chosen, laying the blanket on the soft grass. I motion for her to sit before speaking.

"I'm going to grab us something to drink. They have some spiked cider tonight that smells pretty good. Would you like one?"

Tabi smiles softly at me. "That would be great, Kaz, thanks."

I'm on cloud nine as I walk toward the cider stand, eager to get back to my date, when a shrill voice assaults my eardrums.

"Kaz-ron!" My name is drawn out and whined in the fakest sweet voice you can imagine. I know exactly who's calling for me right now. I turn toward the voice and nearly sigh in frustration.

Emily.

I've successfully avoided the harpy for the last few months. We dated briefly a few years ago, but by date two I knew we weren't compatible. Emily is pretty enough—nothing near Tabitha's beauty—but she is incredibly needy. Don't get me wrong, I want to pamper a partner and love feeling needed, but it felt like every other comment out of her mouth was something self deprecating, as if she needed reassurance. Or she just wanted to bask in compliments.

Also, her voice grates on my nerves. Yes, I am fully aware that's shallow, but can you imagine spending the rest of your life with someone who makes you cringe whenever they talk? We never went on a third date, but Emily hasn't gotten the hint and I'm horrible at confrontation, so I've just avoided the issue altogether. That's come back to bite me in the ass tonight, though.

Emily's wing grazes my shoulder as she comes to stand in front of me, blocking my path.

"Kaz'ron! Oh my gods, what are you doing here? You should have told me you were coming, silly!" She playfully pushes my shoulder as she simpers. I look back toward Tabitha and find her staring at us with furrowed brows. Shit.

Determination fills me, and I prepare to tell Emily once and for all that we are never happening. There is no way I'm letting her ruin my chances with Tabi. I can be firm, but kind. I *can*.

"I'm on a date with Tabitha." The words come out rushed and not at all as confident as I wanted them to. To emphasise my point, I wave my hand awkwardly in the direction of the sweet human woman waiting for me.

The harpy's expression falls before turning petulant. She sends a menacing glare at Tabi, stomps a clawed foot, and storms off with a little *harrumph*.

That didn't go as smoothly as I planned, but when does anything? At least Emily is clear on where I stand and Tabi can rest assured I'm not interested in the interfering harpy. Taking a deep breath, I smile at my date and turn to continue to the cider stand.

There's no line, so I walk right up to the window and am greeted by Hudson, a new guy in town.

"Hey Kaz'ron! What can I get ya?" he greets me happily.

"Two spiked ciders, Hudson, thanks. Oh, and maybe some of those cream cheese danishes." They're a new item Phillipa just made for Grim's bakery, I bet Tabi will like those. It isn't long before Hudson hands me the cups and a small bag through the window, leaning forward conspiratorially, a mischievous shine in his eyes. Oh no.

"Did I just hear you tell Emily that you're here with Tabitha? On *a date*?" he whisper-yells.

"Yep, sure am," I reply, just wanting to end this interaction and get back to said date.

His eyebrows hit his hairline. "A *date* date? Like, *you're dating and she's off the market* kind of date?"

Is it really that hard to believe? Way to take a crowbar to the knees of a male's confidence. Instead of revealing my inner wince, I simply say, "Yes, a date date."

Hudson whistles. "Look at you go, man. She's so hot."

A growl leaves my lips before I can stop it, something hot and possessive rising inside me listening to him objectify Tabitha like that. I mean, he's right, she is hot. But he shouldn't be looking at her that way. *She's mine.*

Before I can unpack *that* alpha-male reaction, I turn and walk away from the cider stand, shoulders stiff, barely stopping myself from crushing the flimsy paper cups I'm still holding.

When I get back to Tabitha, she reaches for one of the cups, her nose scrunching up adorably. "Thank you, Kaz. You okay?"

I plop down on the blanket beside her before I answer. "Yeah, just glad to be back here with you."

That softens her features and gets me a genuine smile again. Before either of us can say something else, a screech rips from the speakers, followed by the mayor's voice. The whole crowd flinches.

"Good evening, Ghostlight Falls! And welcome to ninety's night! It's time to travel back thirty or so years and relive your youth. Please welcome *The Holey Wonders!*"

The crowd claps, but Tabi leans into me. "The ninety's weren't thirty years ago, right? 1995 was like, ten years ago max. Don't tell me otherwise, let me live in this delusion."

We both laugh, then stay close as the band begins to play. Tabitha sings along, head bopping back and forth to the beat. My off-key voice doesn't need to ruin the moment so I don't join in, content to watch her enjoy herself.

The band plays mostly upbeat hits, but then shifts gears to some slower ballads. Suddenly, Tabi scrambles and changes position, moving between my legs with her back to my chest. I wrap an arm around her midsection reflexively, momentarily stunned as she wiggles to get comfortable. Her head tips up and back to look at me.

"Is this ok?" she asks.

"Uh, yeah. More than ok," I manage to reply. Content with that answer, she watches the band again, her posture slowly relaxing until she's nearly melded to my body. It's perfect.

CHAPTER 6
TROUBLEMAKER
TABI

The night air is cool but Kaz's body keeps me warm. He's so comfortable to cuddle with, large enough that I feel like I won't crush him. I've always loved a partner with a soft belly. Dad-bods are in and I am so here for it.

I'm not a small woman. I'm comfortable with my curves, but having a partner that doesn't make me feel 'large' is my preference. As confident in my appearance as I am, insecurity will always rear its ugly head if given the chance.

Kaz makes me feel at ease. He's a little tense behind me, though, so I readjust a little. As my ass shifts closer to his groin, a soft whimper leaves him.

Oh. *Ohhhhh*.

He's not uncomfortable. He's hard.

Well, I guess that still means he's uncomfortable. I

have to hold back a giggle at my lame joke. The music picks back up again with a pop song, and a wicked idea comes to me.

I wiggle my hips to the beat, small movements at first. As the song goes on, my hip rolls become more pronounced. And if I maybe push back a little more than necessary once in a while, grazing his hard cocks? Well, who can blame a girl? The temptation is too strong.

Kaz's grip tightens on my waist, his lips come to my ear. "You keep that up, troublemaker, and one of two things are going to happen. You're gonna make me come in my pants here in front of everyone, and I'm going to have to punish you for it. Or I'm going to drag you into the woods and rut you against a tree."

I inhale sharply, pausing my movements to consider. I knew I was playing with fire, but I didn't expect such dirty words to come from shy Kaz'ron's mouth. I'm no stranger to a romp in the woods, but there are a lot of people around right now, and I'm not sure I can be quiet. Plus, something tells me I'd really enjoy Kaz's *punishment.*

Biting my lip, I move again, grinding against him. My hand covers his, then slowly drags it up to the underside of my breast. His breathing picks up, his hips shunting forward to meet my movements. He grasps my hips and pulls me tight against him as he freezes, then groans low against my neck.

His panting turns to a low chuckle, and he scrapes pointed teeth against my skin just below my ear. "Oh, you are so going to pay for that. I should slide my fingers under this sexy little outfit and make you come right here in front of everyone, but I don't want any of these assholes to see your pleasure."

Instead of packing up to leave, Kaz settles a possessive grip on my waist to watch the rest of the show. My clit throbs from his threat, but he doesn't make a move to touch me lower. The bastard is going to make me wait.

It's pure torture sitting through the second half of the band's set, and when it finally ends, I'm positive a light breeze could set me off. We pack our things, haphazardly rolling the blanket into a crumpled ball, shooting heated glances at each other.

The walk back to my place is a crime against my pussy, each step reminding me how turned on I am and how very little I've come so far. Like, zero. Not at all. It's unfair.

"Did you know that like most supernaturals, demons have a heightened sense of smell?" Kaz's question seems to come out of left field, until I realize what he's implying. My cheeks blaze red.

"That's right," he continues, "I can smell how aroused you are. How *frustrated* you are. And how so very wet you are."

I shoot him a wide-eyed glare. I thought Kaz'ron

was a nice male. Turns out he's actually a teasing asshole. One I am going to jump as soon as we cross my threshold.

We reach my door and my hands shake as I fumble the keys, attempting to get the right one in the lock. It doesn't help that my demon is peppering kisses along my nape, his body pushed against my back.

Finally managing to get it open and push through, Kaz'ron is on me in an instant. He whirls me around and slams my back against my now closed door, immediately crushing his lips to mine in a brutal kiss. We're both frantic, out of our minds with lust, and lacking the finesse you'd usually try to show on a first date. No, it's sloppy, and wet, and *hot*.

"Fuck, Tabi. I've wanted you for so long," Kaz admits against my lips in between kisses. He moves to my neck as I answer.

"Y-you have? Why didn't you say something? Oh, gods!" I moan when Kaz traces his tongue around my earlobe and punctuates it with a sharp nip, his hips thrusting against mine.

He doesn't answer right away, instead kissing his way down my body, dragging his tongue across my cleavage. My back arches, pushing my breasts into his eager palms as he traces the hem of my romper, teasing like he may pull it down and give me what I so desperately want.

"You are so out of my league it isn't funny," Kaz

says. "But I'm also not stupid, so if you give me a chance to please you, I'm going to take it. *Holy Fuck.*" He curses when he finally frees my breasts and sees them bare. His eyes are locked onto my piercings, the bars through my nipples are easy to see with how hard they are.

His fingers graze each one, tentatively at first, until he hears my moans of pleasure when he tugs slightly. Suddenly he's bent down, taking one nipple into his mouth and laving the piercing with his tongue. He rolls it and then nips it between his teeth, and I'm making noises I'm sure will embarrass me later, but right now I can't be bothered to care.

"Never played with something like these before." Both hands knead and play with my tits as he stares into my eyes with his dark, heated gaze. "Can you come just from nipple play?"

"I-I haven't before." I admit.

Kaz's smile turns predatory. "We'll have to test that theory later. Right now," Kaz puts his shoulder against my middle and hauls me over it before I realize what's happening. "It's time to mete out that punishment you earned."

He carries me to my bedroom, putting me down so we are both standing at the foot of the bed. He kisses me again, his hands wandering my body, reaching my ass and sliding under the fabric of my romper to squeeze the globes roughly.

"Bend over the bed, troublemaker."

I comply immediately, laying my top half on the soft surface, presenting my ass to my demon. He runs his hands along my back and up my thighs, searching for a way to gain access to my skin. He tries pulling the legs of the romper up, but they won't go high enough. When he can't find a waistband or zipper, he growls in frustration.

"How the fuck do you get this contraption off? If you don't want me to tear it, I'm gonna need your help." He gripes.

As hot as it is in my smut books when the main character's clothes are ripped off in a fit of passion, I like this outfit and it seems like it'd kill the mood. Giggling as I stand, I slide the straps over my arms and shimmy the whole thing down over my hips, leaving it to pool at the ground by my feet. Before Kaz asks again, I dutifully lay back over the bed, resuming my previous position.

Kaz groans, his hand finally stroking bare skin. "Have you ever been spanked before?"

"Yes." I whimper.

"Did you like it?" he asks.

"Yes."

Without any more conversation, a hand slaps my cheek, leaving behind a pleasant burn after the initial sting. Kaz leans over my back until his mouth is at my ear. "Okay?"

It's sweet he's checking in, but this demon has no idea how not vanilla I am. This is more than okay. I nod, simply answering with, "more."

"Give me a color. Green if you're good, yellow if you need me to slow down, red if you need me to stop," he says, then peppers my ass with two more slaps for good measure.

"I didn't expect you to be so kinky—ah!" I cry out when he smacks me several times in quick succession, not as hard, but enough to make me pay attention. Then he's soothing the sting with his palms, pulling apart my asscheeks to see me dripping onto the bed.

"You do like this, don't you?" he murmurs. Then he's on me like a starved man. He licks my slit, shoving his tongue into my core, then circling my clit. My fists grip the sheets in surprise and pleasure. The sounds echoing in the room are obscene, my body beginning to tingle as it climbs toward the peak.

Two thick fingers push into me and pump against my g-spot, making my legs tremble as I moan his name. Then Kaz wraps his lips around my clit and sucks. That sends me over the edge, screaming his name and pushing back against his face and fingers, riding out my orgasm.

Kaz slips his fingers from my pussy and gently rolls me to my back as I come down from my high. My eyelids are heavy, my body sated like never before. I blink up at him sleepily when he shifts my body up the bed and under the covers.

"What about you?" I ask guiltily. I am exhausted after he ripped that epic orgasm from my body, but I can't leave him hanging out to dry.

Kaz kisses me gently. "Trust me, I enjoyed that as much as you did."

When he tucks me in, I realize he's still fully clothed. I sit up on my elbows to question him. "Wait, are you leaving? You don't want to stay?"

He smiles and kisses my forehead. Damn it, he knows every woman's secret weakness: forehead kisses. "I have to take care of Arlo, he hasn't been fed and is needier than a dog sometimes. I didn't expect, uh, us to get this far tonight. Not that I'm complaining!" He rushes to add when he realizes he sounds disappointed. "But maybe you could come over to my place next Friday? A movie date?"

The sleep is closing in, but I manage to agree before I succumb to my dreams.

CHAPTER 7

SEXT ME, BABY

KAZ'RON

"**A**rlo! Fuckin' eh, buddy. You're a godsdamn turtle, how can you get in my way so stealthily?" The creature in question just looks at me like I'm the idiot. I can practically hear him saying, *don't blame me, I have a frickin balloon tied to my shell. You weren't paying attention.*

And he'd be right. I've been daydreaming constantly since my date with Tabi Saturday night. When I awoke the next day, I still had the taste of her on my tongue. I'm still in shock that things got that hot and heavy on our first date—at all really. I don't know what came over me, but when I realized she was teasing me on purpose, deliberately rubbing against my cocks to torture me, it's as if a switch flipped. All the filthy things I wanted to say to her came pouring out of my mouth, and she fucking *loved* it.

That goddess made me come in my pants like a horny college male—twice. I didn't tell her about the second time, when I came just from eating her out and making her gush on my face. A male's ego can only survive so many hits, and she knew she sent me over the edge at the concert.

I dodge Arlo and walk behind the counter, settling in for the slow afternoon. The store had a rush at lunch, but now everyone is back at work or school and I'm left here with my immoral thoughts of the curvy woman and her surprise nipple piercings. Annnd, there go my cocks again. I don't think they've been fully soft since I left Tabi's house.

As if she knows I'm thinking about her, my phone chimes with a text.

TABI:

Image unavailable in preview

My phone doesn't show messages on the lock screen, too many prying eyes around the shop and I tend to leave it on the counter. Eagerly, I swipe open the message thread and nearly drop the device.

A photo fills my screen. Tabi is taking a mirror selfie, but she's completely naked. Her soft skin and curves are nearly all on display, but she's placed a single finger in front of her strategically, hiding the cleft of her cunt and her nipples from view. Well, most of her nipples. I can still see one of those fucking barbells I know run right through the taut nubs. Her lips are slightly parted in a pout, and as I zoom in I realize she isn't *totally* naked. She still has on her sexy little glasses that give me innumerous naughty librarian fantasies.

She's looking directly at me through the camera, that one finger taunting me. I can imagine her shaking it at me as she scolds me. After about forty-five seconds, another text comes through while I'm still staring in a stupor.

> TABI:
>
> I miss you.
>
> Are you busy tonight? Not sure I can wait til Friday. *winky face*

Is she kidding? I'm never fucking busy, and even if I were, I would clear my schedule in a heartbeat if she wanted to see me. She could demand I come do her laundry and I would be there lickity split, asking what type of detergent she prefers. She wants me to hand-wash her unmentionables? I'll thoroughly enjoy scrubbing those babies clean—especially after I've helped make a mess of them.

What the fuck do I say back? It's not like I can send some sexy selfie, too. I mean, I don't even know that I can take a sexy selfie, and no one wants unsolicited dick pics, even though those are by far some of my strongest assets. Remembering she liked my dirty talk before, I decide to just go for it.

KAZ:

Is my troublemaker ready to be bad?

No, nope. Delete that, try again. That sounds like the opening to a bad porno.

KAZ:

You've been a naughty girl sending photos like that…

Oh gods, no. Seriously, why am I so bad at this?

KAZ:

Fuck, troublemaker. You have me hard at work right now. The only thing I have planned tonight is to get your sexy body underneath mine so we can pick up where we left off.

Ok, sent. That's better. I look around the empty shop and realize something critical. I'm the owner, and I can close whenever I want, for whyever I want. And right now, I want to go home and get ready for Tabi to come over and blow my mind. Maybe rub one or two out before she gets here so I don't embarrass myself when I sink my cocks into her wet heat. I shoot off one more message.

Kaz: Closing up early, come over whenever you're ready.

Quickly, I count the till and sweep faster than I ever have before, then rush out the door, locking it up behind me. Tonight can't come soon enough.

CHAPTER 8

R⬤MATES, AMIRITE?

TABI

My hands shake as I knock on Kaz'ron's door. I'm not sure what possessed me to send that nude earlier today. I was just out of the shower and felt hot when I looked in the mirror. It took the better part of the morning for me to get the courage to actually text it to Kaz. When he didn't respond right away, I was worried I over-stepped, or he didn't like what he saw. But then he sent back that message that got me even more hot and bothered.

I'd like to think he closed up shop early because he is just as excited for this as I am.

I knock twice, then step back on the threshold. When the door opens, I'm greeted by both Kaz and Arlo, the latter wagging his little turtle tail like he's excited to see me. Arlo headbutts my shin with his little horns, pushing against me like a cat might when they want scratchies.

Kaz bends down and picks him up, placing the turtle behind him. "Let the pretty lady get in the house, Arlo. She's here to see me, not you."

I raise a brow as I step inside. "You sure about that? He is awfully cute. And he's excited to see me."

The door shuts and Kaz pulls me into his arms, kissing me soundly before gripping my ass and pulling me against him. His hard cocks press into my belly as he growls, "I'd say I'm more than a little excited to see you, too."

I'm about ready to let this demon take me right here on the floor, but Kaz pulls back, adjusts his crotch and leads me to the couch like he didn't just kiss me stupid. The coffee table has a spread of snacks on it, everything from fruit to what look like mini quiches.

"It's kinda early so I thought we might want a snack while we watch the movie, since dinner is a couple hours yet," Kaz explains as he takes a seat on the couch. He looks at me, his eyes willing me to sit next to him, so I do.

"This is so sweet, Kaz. Thank you." I grab what looks like a slice of peach and lean back, taking a bite. The fruit is ripe and juice explodes on my tongue, some fluid dripping down my chin and fingers. Leave it to me to make a mess in the first five minutes. My tongue darts out to lick the juice off my lips, then I suck my fingers into my mouth to clean those off, too. Kaz is completely silent, his body rigid next to mine. When I finally glance at him, he looks ready to pounce.

"Kaz? Is everything okay?" I squirm a little when he doesn't answer, or even move. Did I piss him off?

"Fuck it."

That's the only warning I get before Kaz is on me, gripping my hips and dragging me into his lap. His hand slides into my hair, fingers gripping the strands as he drags my face to his.

"I was trying to be patient," he says between kisses, "but you had to go licking those lithe fingers, sucking them into your mouth and making me imagine what your plump lips would look like wrapped around my cock."

A lewd moan crawls up my throat when he pulls my head back and licks a stripe down my neck. My hips move on their own, grinding down on his lap, seeking friction. His hand leaves my hair to hold onto my ass, and he helps grind me back and forth over his hardness, thrusting up against my needy pussy on each pass.

"Kaz! Fuck, I—"

"Come for me, Tabi. I want to see your face as you fall apart." Kaz thrusts up once more and I shatter, dry humping my demon like we're in high school—except with more orgasms. Before he can do anything more, I scramble off his lap onto the floor, kneeling between his legs. My hands shoot forward, scrambling with the button and fly on his jeans until I can reach into his boxers and pull his cock out. Scratch that, cocks. I was right.

"Holy fuck." The curse leaves my lips unbidden when I see that not only does he have two dicks, but they are both heavily pierced, a jacob's ladder running up the underside of each.

Breathing heavy, Kaz apologizes. "Sorry, uh, I should have warned you. But I didn't realize you were going to whip my dicks out like that. It was, ah, a silly thing I had done back in college after a buddy of mine —*shit!*"

His rambling is cut off when I lick him from base to tip on his bottom cock, tongue trailing across each of the bars until I dip it into his slit to taste the salty precum there. Having two shafts to deal with is a new, but not unwelcome, challenge. Sitting up a little higher on my knees, I take his top cock in my mouth, getting it nice and wet before I pull back and spit on the tip. My hand begins to pump that shaft steadily so I can take the other cockhead into my mouth and suck.

"Tabitha, fuck. You don't...shit. I don't...oh gods. Fuck your mouth is heaven." Kaz seems properly mindblown, which gives me a little ego boost. Feeling playful, I pop my mouth off his cock and replace it with my free hand so I'm pumping both shafts simultaneously.

"Are you supposed to be talking about heaven as a demon? I feel like hell is more fun."

Kaz sits up and growls, but cuts off abruptly and whips his gaze to the floor. Following his line of sight, I burst out laughing when I see Arlo there, glaring up at his owner, one foot pawing at his calf. My demon just stares, stunned, then scrambles to stand. Bending down to pick up the creature, he holds him in one hand and holds his pants up with the other.

"Sorry buddy, you gotta go." Kaz deposits Arlo into a room off the hallway, then shuts the door. I'm still laughing when he returns, until he drags me off my knees, pressing me into the couch with his body over mine.

"Gods, you're perfect," he murmurs.

I look up at him. "Why?"

"That little asshole could have ruined our night, but you just laughed instead. Most people would have let it kill the mood," he explains.

I reach down, cup his crotch and squeeze. "You think anything can stop me from trying two cocks for the first time? I've seen them, and I want them. Now."

He groans, then there is a flurry of movement as we undress each other, clothes thrown all over the living room with no regard as to where they land. When we're finally naked, Kaz takes his seat on the couch again and urges me to straddle him. I rock over him, his lower cock between my lips getting drenched in my slit. His top cock hits my clit each time and, fuck that's so good.

"Can't wait. Need you now," I tell him before I raise up on my knees. Kaz grips his lower cock and notches the head at my entrance. I look at him questioningly.

He chuckles. "We gotta work you up to taking both of my cocks, troublemaker. We'll start with one, then maybe work up to me fucking this cunt and your perfect ass at the same time. Or squeezing both into your pussy..."

Kaz trails off as I sink down onto him, each barbell slipping past my entrance a new, thrilling sensation. As soon as I'm fully seated, I start to ride him, using his shoulders as leverage. One cock in my pussy is more than enough for now, especially when the other rubs against my clit on every glide.

My demon lets me use him, laving my nipples with his talented tongue as my pussy tightens around his shaft. My orgasm hits me out of nowhere, hard and fast, just like our fucking. Kaz grunts, my channel trying to milk the cum from his balls, but he doesn't give in yet.

Before I finish coming, he lays me down and pulls out. His head pushes between my thighs and he sucks my clit. I grip his horns, holding on for dear life as he devours me. Kaz growls.

"Those are sensitive, troublemaker, and I don't

want to come anywhere other than in your tight cunt this time."

Feeling bratty, I give them a stroke and Kaz cries out. Almost in retaliation, two fingers roughly spear into me and my orgasm builds again. This one feels different. Kaz finger fucks me ruthlessly, changing the angle until he hears me keen, then pummeling my g-spot non-stop. He pushes on my mons with his other hand, and I realize what he's trying to do.

"Kaz, I can't. I've never...I can't!" I wail to him as I try to squirm away. He holds fast.

"Yes you fucking can, and you will. Soak my fucking face, Tabitha. I want to be covered in your cum before I fill you with mine."

My back arches and my head thrashes as he brings me to the edge again. A pressure unlike anything I've felt before builds in my core. I'm about to protest again when Kaz growls.

"Give. It. To. Me." Each word is punctuated by a thrust of his fingers, and this time when he latches his mouth to my clit, I let go. Sure enough, my orgasm is accompanied by a gush of wetness, a scream ripping from me as I come harder than I ever have, soaking Kaz's face just like he demanded.

CHAPTER 9
DOUBLE DEES

KAZ'RON

My knees creak as I rise from the floor, but I couldn't care less. I'll abuse my joints every day if it means I get to see Tabi shatter for me like she just did. Her legs are trembling and she's breathing heavily, eyes closed and body limp.

I knew she could squirt, even if she didn't think she could. And fuck, it was just as hot as I imagined.

Running my hands up her thighs, my fingers trace patterns lightly along her midsection, then up to her chest. My body covers hers as I pepper kisses along her jaw, waiting for her to come back to me before we continue. I desperately want to sink one of my cocks into her, but I need her to look at me while I do it.

Slowly, her eyes flutter open, and I grip the base of my cocks, rubbing the heads through her slick to coat them. Tabi mewls, arching her hips to meet mine, so I notch the head of one to her entrance. I push the head past her tight ring of muscle, the pop satisfying as her needy cunt sucks me in. She squeezes me as each barbell slips inside, a deep moan leaving both of us once I'm fully seated.

Too worked up to wait, I pull out and slam back in, again and again. My top cock, slick with her cum, rubs her clit on each pass. She's discovering exactly why I got both shafts pierced to begin with. My pleasure comes from pleasuring my partner, as is evidenced by me shooting my load just from licking her sweet cunt.

We clash together, all passion and groans and heat, but I need to get closer, deeper. This burgeoning connection between us seems like more than just physical attraction. Demons don't have fated mates, but damn if that's not what this feels like.

Tabi whimpers when I pull out, switching positions so I'm lying behind her on the couch, her supple body cradled tight against mine. My other cock needs attention, and when I push into her again from behind, she sighs happily. At this angle, I hit her g-spot every time I pump my hips forward, but I want to fill her completely.

My left hand grips the nape of her neck, holding her tight as my right arm hooks under her leg, lifting to her chest it to open her sex wide. Her arousal drips down my balls, and I hope she ruins the leather with her wetness. A reminder of the best night of my fucking life.

I rock into her with deep, powerful thrusts, my rhythm faltering as her core begins fluttering around me. Tabitha tilts her face toward mine in a silent plea for a kiss, and who am I to deny her?

Our lips meet, and she fucks my mouth with her tongue while I fuck her sweet pussy. Something clenches in my chest, and I realize it's my heart. I've had a crush on this amazing woman for the better part of a year, but this moment just solidifies the fact that she's *mine*.

I've never felt the depth of emotion during sex as quickly as I have with this woman. My thrusts slow, and we aren't just fucking, we're making love. Gods, I love the dichotomy this woman gives me. She's my dirty little slut one moment, and my wholesome lover the next.

The familiar tingle starts in the base of my spine, and I know I won't last much longer. Breaking the kiss, my forehead presses against hers.

"Tabi, I'm s-so close. Where do you want me to come, baby?" I manage to ask.

"In me," she moans. "I'm on birth control, *please*, Kaz, fill me up with your cum."

See what I said about her two sides? Her pleading does it, and three strokes later I'm holding myself deep as I empty my seed into her. The cock not filling her explodes along her soft belly and swollen clit, and I can't help but to take my hand and smooth it into her skin, claiming her thoroughly.

For a while, we're silent, just basking in each other. Then Tabi giggles. I look at her in confusion.

"Did you...did you just sexile poor Arlo?" she snorts. The ridiculousness of the comment sends me into a fit of laughter, also, and it just feels so good. So easy and right.

Gods, this woman is everything, and I'm going to do my damndest to keep her.

EPILOGUE

TABI

"Sooo, how are things going with you and your kinky demon?" My best friend teases me through the phone.

"I never should have given you so much detail," I grumble.

Hannah gasps, "Don't you dare threaten me, missy! Not all of us get to be double-dicked down by a dirty-talking demon, I have to live vicariously through you! My man only has one dick, and it isn't even *pierced*!"

A chuckle escapes me at her mock outrage. She has a point, Kaz'ron is...everything. We've been inseparable since our second date—which really ended up just being a fuck-fest. Not that I'm complaining, the male is *experienced*, if you know what I'm saying.

I've taken to working from Ruff 'N Tumble, the animals a nice distraction from my home office. Mochi, the foxkin, is my favorite—don't tell Arlo. I have a soft spot for her since her antics brought Kaz and I together, finally. Plus, she's a great cuddler. Arlo is adorable, but that hard teal shell isn't exactly fluffy. Anyway, he's a daddy's boy through and through.

The bell tinkles over the shop door, and I look up, expecting to see my handsome demon walking in. He ran out to grab us lunch and left me in charge of the store. Instead, Oliver, the postman, walks in and sets an envelope on the counter in front of me.

I stare down at the envelope in confusion, but by the time I glance back up, Oliver is gone.

"Hmm, that's odd," I mutter to myself, picking up the fancy mail. The envelope itself is a cream color, the paper reminiscent of old parchment. It's addressed to me in fancy calligraphy, a red and gold wax seal along the closure.

Opening it, I pull out what turns out to be a folded map of Ghostlight Falls. I love this little town and all the quirky residents in it. This map, however, has a path drawn that leads to the park. A simple handwritten note at the bottom catches my eye.

Come find me, troublemaker. -K

Butterflies flutter in my chest. My demon is always

romantic, but this is next level. What could he be planning? He obviously sent this note, so it stands to reason he's ok with me closing up shop. It isn't like we've had any customers since he left. I wonder if that's by design.

Scooping up Mochi, I let her perch on my shoulder as I lock the door and begin following the path laid out on the map in my hands. It isn't the most direct route to the park, considering it's basically right next door, and I have to imagine that's on purpose.

The route takes me away from my destination at first, and as I pass by For the Plot, the local book shop, Bea smiles at me and hands me a stack of blind-wrapped books. I'm not sure what they are, until I pause on the sidewalk and read the note attached.

More research for you, I love each new experience you find for us to try. - K

Bea looks at me knowingly, and I thank her, blushing bright red as I keep walking. Just a bit later, Grim's bakery comes into view. The green shopkeeper bustles out to hand me a cupcake, another handwritten note on the top of the box.

Dessert for you, but I want mine later. -K

Good gods, has Kaz let the whole town in on our

insatiable sexual appetites? I'm not shy, but damn. Based on the awkward look Grim sends me before scurrying back inside, my hypothesis is correct.

I'm gonna strangle that male.

Sheet-y Stationary is next, but there isn't a shop-keeper waiting for me this time. Instead, there is a basket full of sealed letters on a small round table in front of the shop. Each one has my name on it, and a different date.

I set my bounty down and open the first one. Tears sting my eyes when I see it's a love letter from Kaz, from the week we started dating. Examining the rest, I realize he's written me one nearly every other day since we first fell into each other's arms. He's been hiding these from me for months.

Placing the letter, books, and cupcake in the basket, I grab it and scurry to the park. Screw this scavenger hunt, I need to see my handsome, sweet, sexy demon right now. Luckily, the map leads me to the park next, anyway.

Anticipation grips me as I finally arrive and catch sight of Kaz. He's dressed up nicely in a fitted suit, a bouquet of flowers in his hands that looks just like the one he brought me on our first date. On his left stands Arlo. I squint as I get closer. Is he wearing a tiny bow tie?

Of course he is. Gods the pair is so damn cute.

I nearly forgot the foxkin on my shoulders until

she barks out a greeting and hops down to join the turtle on the ground.

"Hi," I breathe out when I reach Kaz.

He smiles lovingly at me, handing me the flowers. "Hi."

Once the flowers are in my grip, Kaz fidgets nervously, one hand in his pants pocket.

"What—" I start to ask but am cut off by the male in front of me dropping to one knee on the soft grass. "Oh!"

"Tabitha, I...I'm not good at grand gestures..." he starts, and I scoff.

"Really? Because all of this," I say, waving at the basket, "seems to prove otherwise."

He chuckles. "I just, uh, hold on." Kaz fumbles something out of his pocket and I nearly pass out when I realize it's a small, velvet box.

"I'm not good at grand gestures," he starts again, "but you make me want to give you everything. You deserve so much more than I can offer, but I'm a selfish male, and I hope you'll let me keep you."

Arlo butts his horns into Kaz's thigh and Mochi yips in protest. "Hah, sorry. *We* hope you'll let *us* keep you. I love you, Tabi. Will you marry me?"

I launch myself at him, kissing him deeply. Kaz lets out a soft oomph as his back hits the ground. When I finally pull back, he tucks a strand of hair behind my ear.

"So, is that a yes?" he asks.

"Of course it's a yes, you dolt!" I laugh through the words as Arlo and Mochi join our cuddle pile on the ground. "There's no one else I'd rather take a tumble with."

SECOND EPILOGUE

KAZ'RON

If you'd have asked me ten years ago where I thought I'd be now, it sure wouldn't be covered in mud, being dragged by my now-fiance towards my house after we dropped off our animal babies at Ruff 'N Tumble.

After she said yes and I slid that ring on her finger, Tabitha flat out told me she wanted me to, and I quote, "fill all my holes with your studded cocks and ride me hard until I'm dripping with your cum."

Gods, I fucking love this woman.

We're barely through the door before she's on me, dropping to her knees in the hall and tearing at my jeans to get them undone. Before I can say a word, she has both my cocks out, one deep in her throat while the other brushes against her tits.

"Fuck! Troublemaker, holy gods your fucking mouth. Slow down...or...fuuuck."

Tabi doesn't slow. She slips her mouth off my cock and drops to the other, dragging her tongue along my piercings before taking me inside. Her soft hand works the cock she already soaked with her spit, and she sucks me hard, like she's trying to milk me dry.

"Tabi, sweetheart, I'm gonna come if you don't stop now." I groan as I feel my orgasm speeding toward me like a freight train. My troublemaker looks up at me with a wicked glint in her eye, then grasps both cocks in her fists and wraps her lips around both heads, flicking her tongue across the tips where precum has gathered. She pumps and sucks and I'm a goner, yelling out her name as I find my release and spill down her throat. My woman swallows every last drop.

I think I black out a little.

When my vision returns, my chest is heaving, and Tabi is pulling her shirt off as she rises from the floor.

"Kaz, I need you to fuck me. Right now," she demands. She spins to shimmy her shorts over her wide hips, then bends sensually at the waist as she drags them down her thick thighs. Her pussy is already soaking wet, and I'm mesmerized by the slick pink folds she's showing off.

Until a glint catches my eye.

No. Fucking. Way.

Tabitha wiggles her ass, and a jewel winks at me from above her cunt. She's got a plug in. I've died and gone to hell. Looks like I wasn't the only one with a surprise planned today.

"You weren't kidding when you said you wanted me to fill all your holes were you?" I rasp.

She walks toward the couch, throwing me a coy look over her shoulder. "My *fiancé* has two gorgeous cocks, and I have every intention of taking them both for a ride today. If you're up for it, that is."

A growl rips from me and I stalk after her, crashing into her back and pulling her flush against me. One hand grips her throat while the other dives straight between her legs to spank her clit.

"Are you trying to drive me into a rut? You want me to fuck you in both your tight holes until you can't walk straight? Because you're playing with fire, troublemaker." I soothe the sting on her clit with the pads of my fingers, spreading her slick around in circles.

Tabi moans but grits out, "Show me what you've got, old man."

That does it. I shove two fingers into her cunt, then pick her up, her weight pushing them as deep inside her as they'll go. I scissor them to stretch her out as I walk her to the couch, roughly shoving her to her knees and bending her over the cushion when we get there.

Dropping to kneel behind her, I grip her hair to

yank her head back and begin fucking her with my fingers roughly. My thumb rocks over the plug in her ass, jiggling it on every thrust.

"Fuck! Kaz, I'm so close!" she keens. I remove my fingers immediately, causing her to whine in frustration.

Stripping off the rest of my clothes, I tell her, "I told you you were playing with fire, troublemaker. Now you don't get to come unless it's on both my cocks. Lube?"

Tabi huffs, but points to the end table. Sliding open the drawer, I see the small bottle. My female was prepared.

With a husky chuckle, I tip the bottle over her ass, dripping lube down her crack and over the gem covering her tight hole. Snapping the lid closed, I set it aside, then gently tug on the plug, rocking it back and forth, then spinning it. Tabi drops her forehead to the cushions and groans. Unable to wait much longer, I pull the plug out with a soft pop, and replace it with my fingers, pushing the lube deep to make sure she's ready to take me.

"Kaz, I'm ready. Please!" Tabi cries, shoving her hips back to ride my fingers. My dicks are hard again, so I grab the bottle once more, dribbling a generous amount over my cocks and slicking them up with my palm.

Settling behind her once more, I notch one head at

the entrance to her cunt and grip the base of my top cock, guiding it to her asshole.

"You ready? Don't forget your colors," I remind her, then I push forward slowly. It's a tight fit as I fill her body, but I manage to slide in to the hilt without too much resistance.

I hold myself still for a moment, letting her adjust, and letting myself catch my breath before I come on the first stroke. I haven't fucked someones ass in years, not since my boyfriend in college, and never have I filled a woman so completely. The feeling is indescribable.

Tabi begins to squirm, and I take that as my queue to move, pulling back then thrusting deep again. Leaning over my female, I grip under her chin, tipping her head back so I can see her face. Her expression is pure ecstasy as she leans into my touch, rising to her elbows which only arches her back and lets me sink even deeper.

I press a kiss to her temple, showing her how much I adore her even if I'm fucking her like my little slut right now. Tabi's cries become near feral as my pace quickens until I'm slamming into her so hard the couch bangs against the wall. Her body clenches and she peaks, squirting cum all over my balls and the floor as her body fights my intrusion. She's still fluttering from aftershocks when I sink deep and fill her with my release. Hot ropes of cum paint the inside of her ass and cunt, so much it drips out as I thrust lazily through the last echoes of pleasure.

After a few moments I pull out, wincing as her body tries to grip my oversensitive shafts. I lean back against the couch, pulling her with me until she's cradled in my arms.

My hands softly roam her body, soothing her with caring touches after the rough way I took her. Tabi hums happily, eyes closed and body sated.

My fiance mumbles something, but it's too quiet.

"What was that, troublemaker?"

"Do we have to get the creatures, or can we do that again first?" she ekes out.

A belly laugh bursts from me at my insatiable female. I truly am in for a lifetime of trouble, and I wouldn't change a thing.

About the Author

Clover Holloway is the cozier side of Unfortunate Reads, writing steamy monster and omegaverse romance that will leave you swooning and sweating. A long time romance reader turned author, she just can't help but make her stories cozy.

She's an ADHD agent of chaos so her book topics may vary wildly, but you can always expect an HEA. She's an avid fan of traditional millennial customs including craft breweries, monstera plants, and skinny jeans.

You can find all her links at cloverholloway.com, including her Patreon, which is shared with Unfortunate Reads so you get two for one. *Stay lucky!*

ALSO BY AUTHOR

By Clover Holloway

Zero to 69

(co-write with Thea Masen and Kate McDarris)

Welcome to Bone Town

(co-write with Thea Masen)

Slip into Me

READ THE OTHER BOOKS SET IN GHOSTLIGHT FALLS

The Totally Typical Tale of Mappy McMapface

Nicole Parker

Paper and Passion

Thea Masen

Romanced by the Rat

G.M. Fairy

Bread by the Grim

Dakota Cockaday

Cooking Up a Demon

Sabrina Cross

Twi-flight

Luna Cantrip

Taking a Tumble

Clover Holloway

Defined and Defiled

Elsie LePlant

Cirrus About You

Latrexa Nova

Hello, Nurse!

Nicole Parker

Her Wonderful Wonder Belle

Sylvia Morrow

Knot Falling In Love

Kenzie James